D0580020

# Aesop's Fables

*Titles in Derrydale's Illustrated Stories for Children Series*

My Book of Favorite Fairy Tales

Children's Stories from Dickens

American Indian Fairy Tales

The Legend of Sleepy Hollow

Aesop's Fables

Ali Baba and the Forty Thieves and Other Stories

Rip Van Winkle

The Little Mermaid and Other Hans Christian Andersen Fairy Tales

# Aesop's Fables

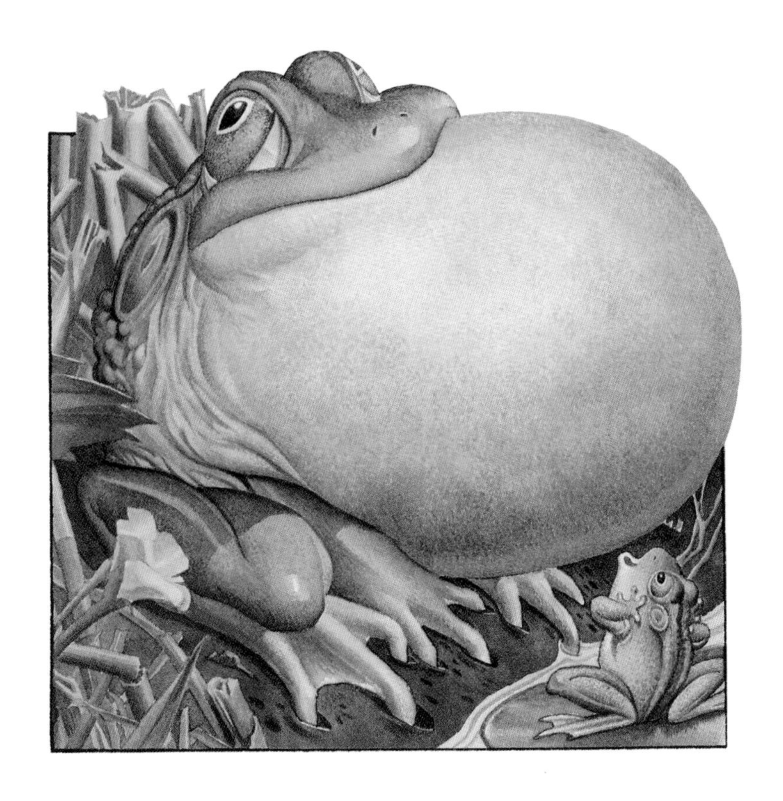

Illustrated by Charles Santore

Derrydale
New York

This 1999 edition is published by Derrydale™,
an imprint of Random House Value Publishing, Inc.,
201 East 50th Street, New York, New York 10022.



Random House
New York • Toronto • London • Sydney • Auckland
http://www.randomhouse.com/

Printed and bound in Singapore

*A CIP catalog record for this book is available from the Library of Congress.*

Aesop's Fables / illustrated by Charles Santore /
Series: Illustrated Stories for Children
ISBN 0-517-20422-3

8 7 6 5 4 3 2 1

# Contents

# Introduction

What if, one day, you looked into your mirror and staring back at you was a wily fox, or maybe a proud lion, a greedy dog, or even a stubborn donkey? This may sound silly, but as you read the stories in this book you will understand—for a fable is like a mirror in which the antics and adventures of animals reflect the wise as well as the foolish behavior of human beings.

People have been telling fables for thousands of years in countries throughout the world. At first glance most fables seem to be simple, clever stories about animals. A boastful hare, for example, stops to rest right in the middle of his race against a plodding tortoise. A scheming fox flatters a crow out of her tasty piece of cheese. But look closer, for fables were created to give *people* useful advice. After all, we're only human! Some days we work hard, other days we're lazy. We can be kind, but we can also be downright mean. A witty fable makes a good mirror.

Who was Aesop, the man who is credited with writing the fables in this book, and how did he become so wise? No one knows for sure, but many stories have been told of his life: Aesop is said to have lived in Greece in the sixth century B.C. That's more than twenty-five hundred years ago. He was a slave, probably from Ethiopia, and was called simply the Ethiop, or Aesop. Some people say he was deformed—humpbacked and ugly—but he was a smart man and a wonderful storyteller. He made up fables to teach people how to behave better. Because of his unusual insights and understanding of right and wrong, Aesop was given his freedom. He traveled far and wide telling his stories, even to the court of the emperor Croesus. But not everyone agreed with Aesop's teachings, and one day, according to legend, he was hurled off a cliff near Delphi, killed by some people who were angry with him.

Aesop's fables lived on and became even more popular as they were passed down by word-of-mouth, from person to person, and from generation to generation, over the centuries. After almost three hundred years, in 300 B.C., the fables of Aesop were written down for the first time, by a Greek politician. Since then many other versions of Aesop's fables have been put into print, with additional fables, from other countries, added as the years went by.

In most of Aesop's fables, animals do the talking, but there are also many others—like The Boy Who Cried "Wolf"—in which people are the heroes or the culprits. You may already know some of the fables in this book. In other cases you may have heard the moral, or saying, that accompanies the fable, but do not know the story behind it. Now you can discover the fables that illustrate such sayings as "Look before you leap," "There are two sides to every question," "Don't count your chickens before they are hatched." In this book you will find eighty-two of Aesop's wonderful fables, and you don't have to look for a lesson to enjoy their timeless wit and wisdom. As you read the fables selected for this new collection, you will also enjoy the stunning color illustrations by Charles Santore. Never before has an artist imbued the animals in Aesop's fables with so much life, vitality, and humor.

NINA ROSENSTEIN

# The Boy Who Cried "Wolf"

A shepherd boy was tending his flock near a village and thought it would be great fun to trick the villagers by pretending that a wolf was attacking the sheep. So he shouted, "Wolf! Wolf!" and when everyone came running to help, he laughed at them for being fooled. He did this more than once, and each time the villagers discovered that they had been tricked, for there was no wolf at all. One day a wolf did come, and he began to attack the sheep. The boy yelled, "Wolf! Wolf!" as loud as he could. But the villagers, thinking he was tricking them once again, paid no attention to his cries for help. And so the wolf killed one sheep after another, until the whole flock was dead.

*People will not believe a liar, even when he tells the truth.*

# The Fox and the Grapes

A hungry fox saw some fine bunches of grapes hanging high up on a vine. "Those grapes look so plump and juicy," said the fox. "I must have them!" The fox did his best to reach the grapes by jumping as far as he could into the air. But it was all in vain, for they were just out of his reach. So he gave up trying and walked away with an air of dignity and unconcern, remarking, "I thought those grapes were ripe, but I see now they are quite sour."

*It's easy to belittle what you cannot have.*

# Jupiter and the Tortoise

The god Jupiter invited all the animals to his wedding celebration. Every one of them came except the tortoise, who did not show up, much to Jupiter's surprise. When Jupiter next saw the tortoise, he asked him why he hadn't come to the party. "I don't like to go out," said the tortoise. "There's no place like home." Jupiter was so annoyed by this answer that he decreed that forever after, the tortoise would have to carry his house upon his back and would never be able to get away from home even if he wished to.

# The Cat and the Birds

A cat heard that the birds in an aviary were feeling sick. He disguised himself as a doctor and went to the aviary, where he inquired about the health of the birds. "We shall do very well," they replied, without letting him in, "when you go back where you came from!"

*A villain may disguise himself, but he will not deceive the wise.*

# The Dog and the Wolf

A dog was lying in the sun before a farmyard gate when a wolf pounced upon him and was going to eat him up. But the dog begged for his life, saying, "You can see how thin I am and what a wretched meal I would make you now. But if you will wait just a few days, my master is going to give me a feast of rich scraps and pickings. I shall get nice and fat, and that will be the time for you to eat me." The wolf thought this was a very good plan and he went away. Sometime afterward he came back to the farmyard and found the dog lying out of reach on the roof of the barn. "Come on down and be eaten," he called. "You remember our agreement?" But the dog said coolly, "My friend, if you ever catch me lying down by the gate again, don't wait for any feast."

# The Lion and the Wild Donkey

A lion and a wild donkey went out hunting together. The donkey, with his superior speed, was to chase down the prey. Then the fearsome lion would take over. The two hunters had great success, but when it was time to share the spoil, the lion split it all into three equal portions. "I will take the first," said he, "because I am King of the Beasts. I will also

take the second, because, as your partner, I am entitled to half of what remains. And as for the third—well, unless you give it to me and take off pretty quickly, the third, believe me, will make you feel very sorry for yourself!"

*You cannot win if you do business with a bully.*

# The Pig and the Sheep

A pig found his way into a meadow where a flock of sheep grazed. The shepherd caught him and was about to carry him off to the butcher's when the pig started to squeal and struggle to get free. The sheep scolded him for making such a fuss and said to him, "The shepherd catches us all the time and drags us off just like that, and we sheep don't make any fuss at all." "No, I suppose you don't," replied the pig, "but my situation and yours are completely different. He only wants you for wool, but he wants me for bacon."

*Don't judge others before you know all the facts.*

# The Dog and the Shadow

A dog was on his way home with a big piece of meat in his mouth. As he crossed a small bridge over a stream, he looked down and saw his own reflection in the water. Thinking it was another dog with an even bigger hunk of meat, he let go of his own supper and jumped in to grab the larger piece. But, of course, he ended up with nothing at all, for his own meat was carried away downstream, and the other was only a shadow.

*When you are greedy, you may lose everything.*

# The Wily Lion

A lion watched a fat bull feeding in a meadow, and his mouth watered when he thought of the delicious feast the bull would make. But the lion did not dare attack, for he was afraid of the bull's sharp horns. Finally, he grew so hungry that he came up with a plan to trick the bull. He went over to the bull in a friendly way and said, "I cannot help saying how much I admire your magnificent figure. What a fine head! What powerful shoulders and thighs! But, my dear friend, what in the world makes you wear those ugly horns? You must find them as awkward as they are unsightly. Believe me, you would do much better without them." The bull was foolish enough to be persuaded by this flattery to have his horns cut off. And without his sharp horns as defense, he fell easy prey to the hungry lion.

*Beware of advice offered by your enemy.*

# The Wild Boar and the Fox

One day a wild boar was in the forest busily sharpening his tusks on a tree trunk when a fox came by. Seeing what the boar was doing, the fox said to him, "Why are you doing that? The hunters are not out today and there are no other dangers around that I can see." "True, my friend," replied the boar, "but the instant my life is in danger I shall need to use my tusks, and there will be no time to sharpen them then."

*Be prepared.*

# The Crow and the Pitcher

A thirsty crow found a pitcher with a couple of inches of water in the bottom, but no matter how hard she tried, she could not reach it with her beak. It seemed as though she would die of thirst. At last she hit upon a plan. She began dropping pebbles into the pitcher. As each pebble was added, the water rose a little higher until it finally reached the brim of the pitcher. And so the clever bird was finally able to quench her thirst.

*Necessity is the mother of invention.*

# The Vain Jackdaw

Jupiter, King of the Gods, decided to appoint a king over the birds. "Tomorrow," he said, "I will select the most beautiful of the birds to be your ruler." The birds all wanted to look their best, so they went to the banks of a stream to prepare themselves—washing and preening their feathers. The jackdaw was there along with the rest. "I am too ugly," he thought. "But perhaps I can fix that." So when all the other birds had gone home, the jackdaw picked up the gaudiest of the feathers that they had dropped and fastened them around his own body. Now he looked fancier and more colorful than anyone else. The next morning, all the birds lined up in front of the palace. Jupiter was about to make the jackdaw king when the rest of the birds jumped upon him, stripped him of his borrowed plumes, and exposed him for the plain creature that he was.

*Don't try to be what you are not.*

# The Fir Tree and the Bramble

A fir tree was boasting to a bramble and said, with some snobbery, "You poor creature, you are of no use at all. Now, look at me: I am useful for all sorts of things, especially when people build houses. They cannot do without my wood." The bramble replied, "Yes, that's surely true. But just wait until they come with axes and saws to cut you down, and then you'll wish you were a poor little bramble and not a big fancy fir!"

# The North Wind and the Sun

The North Wind and the Sun began to argue, each claiming to be stronger than the other. At last they agreed to try their powers upon a traveler to see who could get him to remove his coat. The North Wind tried first. Gathering up all his force for the attack, he came whirling furiously down upon the man and whipped his coat as if to grab it off him in one burst of power. But the harder the wind blew, the more closely the man wrapped his coat around himself. Next it was the turn of the Sun. At first he beamed gently upon the traveler, who soon unbuttoned his coat and walked on with it hanging loosely open. Then the Sun shone brightly in his full strength, and the man, before he had gone many more steps, was happy to take his coat right off and continue on without it.

*Gentle persuasion works better than force.*

# The Eagle and the Roosters

There were two roosters in the same farmyard and they had a fight to decide who should be master. When the fight was over, the beaten one went and hid himself in a dark corner, while the victor flew up onto the roof of the stables and crowed lustily. But an eagle spied him from high up in the sky and swooped down and carried him off. The other rooster came out of his corner and ruled the roost without a rival.

*Pride comes before a fall.*

# The Wolf in Sheep's Clothing

A wolf decided to disguise himself so that he could prey upon a flock of sheep without being caught. So he dressed himself in a sheepskin and slipped among the sheep when they were out at pasture. He completely deceived the shepherd, and when the flock was put back into the pen for the night, the wolf was locked in with them, right where he wanted to be. But as it happened, the shepherd wanted some mutton for dinner that evening. When he came out to the pen, he grabbed the wolf, mistaking him for a sheep, and quickly finished him off with his knife.

*Those who intend to harm others often come to harm themselves.*

# The Fox and the Stork

A sly fox invited a stork to dinner and served her some soup on a large, flat plate. The fox lapped it up with great enthusiasm, but the stork, with her long bill, could not get any of the savory broth. The stork was hungry and upset, but the sly fox just laughed at her. A few days later, the stork invited the fox to dinner. She served him a delicious meal in a pitcher with a long, narrow neck. Her bill fit into the pitcher with ease. So while the stork enjoyed her meal, the fox sat by hungry and helpless, for it was impossible for him to reach the tempting food.

*If you play a trick on a friend, don't be surprised if you are tricked in return.*

# The Wolf and the Lion

A wolf stole a lamb from the flock. He was carrying it off to devour it at his leisure when he met a lion, who seized the lamb and walked off with it. The wolf did not dare to resist, but when the lion had gone some distance he said, "It is most unjust of you to take what's mine away from me like that." The lion laughed and called out in reply, "It was justly yours, no doubt? The gift of a friend, perhaps, eh?"

*You have no right to claim ownership of what is not rightfully yours.*

# Venus and the Cat

A cat fell in love with a handsome young man and begged the goddess Venus to change her into a woman. Venus was very gracious about it and immediately changed the cat into a beautiful maiden. The young man fell in love with her at first sight and they were soon married. One day Venus thought she would like to see whether the cat had changed her habits as well as her appearance, so she let a mouse run loose in the couple's house. Forgetting everything, when the young woman saw the mouse she dashed after it. The goddess Venus was so disgusted that she changed her back again into a cat.

*Changing your looks does not change your nature.*

# The Monkey as King

At a gathering of all the animals, the monkey danced and delighted the others so much that they made him their king. The fox, however, was disgusted at the idea of the monkey as king. The next day the fox found a trap with a piece of meat in it and took the trap with the meat to the monkey, saying, "Here is a dainty morsel I have found, sire. I did not take it myself because I thought it ought to be saved for you, our king. Will you be pleased to accept it?" The monkey reached at once for the meat and was immediately caught in the trap. He bitterly scolded the fox for leading him into danger. But the fox only laughed and said, "Monkey, you call yourself King of the Beasts and haven't more sense than to be tricked like that!"

*Before you choose a leader, consider well what skills make a good one.*

# The Lion and the Mouse

A lion asleep in his lair was awakened by a mouse running over his face. Losing his temper, the lion seized the mouse with his paw and was about to kill her. The mouse was terrified and begged the lion to spare her life. "Please let me go," she cried, "and one day I will repay you for your kindness." The idea of so insignificant a creature ever being able to do anything for him amused the lion so much that he laughed aloud and good-humoredly let her go. But the mouse's chance came, after all.

A few days later, the lion got entangled in a net that had been left as a trap by some hunters. When he discovered that he could not break free, he roared in anger. The mouse recognized the lion's roars and ran to the spot where he was trapped. Immediately the little mouse set to work gnawing the ropes with her teeth. She soon succeeded in setting the lion free. "There!" said the mouse. "You laughed at me when I promised I would repay you, but now you see that even a mouse can help a lion."

*Little friends may prove to be great friends.*

# The Quack Frog

Once upon a time a frog came out from his home in the marshes and proclaimed to all the world that he was a fine physician, skilled in medicines and able to cure all diseases. Among the crowd listening to him was a fox, who called out, "You, a doctor! Why, how can you intend to heal others when you cannot even cure your own lame legs and your blotched and wrinkled skin?"

*Physician, heal yourself.*

# The Peacock and Juno

The peacock was unhappy because he did not have a beautiful voice like the nightingale, so he went to the goddess Juno to complain. "The nightingale's song," he said, "is the envy of all the birds, but whenever I utter a sound everyone laughs." The goddess tried to console him by saying, "It is true that you do not have the power of song, but you are far more beautiful than the other birds. Your neck flashes like an emerald and your tail is splendidly colorful." But the peacock was not satisfied. "What is the use of being beautiful, if one has an ugly voice like mine?" he asked. Then Juno replied, rather sternly, "Fate has given every creature a gift—to you, beauty; to the eagle, strength; to the nightingale, song; and so on to all the rest. You are the only one who is complaining. I suggest that you stop, for if you got your wish, you would soon find something else to be unhappy about."

*Be happy with what you've got.*

# The Fox and the Crow

A fox saw a crow sitting high in a tree with a piece of cheese in her beak. The fox wanted that delicious cheese for himself, so he thought of a plan. Standing under the tree, he looked up and said, "What a noble bird I see above me! Her beauty is without equal, the colors of her feathers exquisite. If her voice is as sweet as her looks are fair, she should be Queen of the Birds." The crow was hugely flattered by this, and just to show the fox that she could sing, she gave a loud caw. Down fell the cheese, of course, and the fox, snatching it up, said, "You have a voice, Madam, I see. What you lack is brains."

*Do not trust flatterers.*

# The Town Mouse and the Country Mouse

A town mouse and a country mouse were acquaintances. One day the country mouse invited his friend to visit him at his home in the fields. When the town mouse arrived, they sat down to a dinner of barleycorns and roots, which had a distinctly earthy flavor. The food was not much to the taste of the guest, who soon said, "My poor dear friend, you live here no better than the ants. Now, you should just see how I eat! My pantry holds a true feast. You must come and stay with me, and, I promise you, you shall live on the fat of the land." So when the town mouse returned to town, he took the country mouse with him and showed him a room full of flour and oatmeal and figs and honey and dates. The country mouse had never seen anything like it and sat down to enjoy the luxuries his friend provided. But before they had begun to eat, the pantry door opened and someone came in. The two mice scampered off and hid themselves in a narrow and exceedingly uncomfortable hole. Presently, when all was quiet, they tiptoed out again, but someone else came in, and off they scuttled again. This was too much for the visitor. "Good-bye," said he. "I'm leaving. You live in the lap of luxury, I can see, but you are surrounded by dangers. I am much happier in my home, where I can enjoy my simple dinner of roots and corn in peace."

*A simple meal eaten in peace*
*is better than the finest food eaten in fear.*

# The Crab and His Mother

An old crab said to her son, "Why do you walk sideways like that, my son? You ought to walk straight." The young crab replied, "Show me how, dear mother, and I'll follow your example." The old crab tried and tried, but her efforts were in vain, for she could not walk straight herself. Then she saw how foolish she had been to find fault with her child.

*Example is the best teacher.*

# Mercury and the Woodsman

A woodcutter was chopping down a tree on the bank of a river when his ax flew out of his hands and fell into the water. Without his ax, the man could not earn a living to feed his family, so he was very upset indeed. Suddenly the god Mercury appeared and offered to help. Mercury dived into the water and brought up an ax made of solid gold. "Is this your lost ax?" he asked the woodcutter. The woodcutter said no, so Mercury dived back into the river and this time brought up a silver ax. "No, that is not mine either," said the woodcutter. Once more Mercury dived into the river, and this time he brought up the missing ax. The woodsman was overjoyed and thanked Mercury warmly. Mercury was so pleased with the man's honesty that he presented him with both the gold ax and the silver ax. When the woodcutter told the story to his friends, one of them was filled with envy. So this other woodcutter went to the bank of the river and let his ax fall into the river. Mercury soon appeared and offered to help. He dived into the water and brought up a gold ax, as he had done before. Without even waiting to be asked whether the ax was his or not, the fellow cried, "That's mine, that's mine," and reached out his hand eagerly for the prize. But Mercury was so disgusted at the man's dishonesty that he not only refused to give him the golden ax, but he also left the man's own ax lying at the bottom of the river.

*Honesty is the best policy.*

# The Fox Without a Tail

A fox was running through the woods when he suddenly fell into a trap. After a struggle he managed to get free, but his bushy tail was sliced right off. The fox was so ashamed of his appearance that he hid in the forest where no one could see him. But then he came up with an idea: perhaps he could persuade the other foxes to part with their tails, too. So he called a meeting of all the foxes. "Brothers," he said, "look at me. I've finally managed to rid myself of that terrible tail. Tails are such ugly things, and besides, they're heavy, and it's tiresome to be always carrying them around with you. You should all get rid of yours." But one of the other foxes said, "My friend, if you hadn't lost your own tail, you would not be so keen on getting us to cut off ours."

*Misery loves company.*

# The Serpent and the Eagle

An eagle swooped down upon a serpent and seized it in his talons, ready to carry it off and devour it. But the serpent was too quick for the eagle and had its coils around him in a moment. The two were locked in a life-and-death struggle when a countryman appeared. He came to the assistance of the eagle and succeeded in freeing him from the serpent. In revenge, the serpent spat some of his poison into the man's water bottle. Hot and tired, the man was about to take a drink when the eagle flew down and knocked the bottle out of his hand, spilling the contents on the ground.

*One good turn deserves another.*

# The Boy and the Nuts

A boy put his hand into a jar of nuts and grabbed as many as his fist could possibly hold. But when he tried to pull his hand out again, he found it was stuck, for the neck of the jar was too small for such a large handful. Unwilling to let go of any of the nuts, yet unable to pull out his hand, the boy burst into tears. A bystander saw the problem and said, "Come on now, don't be so greedy. Be content with half the amount and you'll be able to get your hand out with no trouble at all."

*Do not attempt too much at once.*

# The Stag at the Pool

A thirsty stag went down to a pool to drink. As he bent over the water, he saw his own reflection. "Look how strong and beautiful my antlers are," he said. At the same time he was disgusted at the weakness and skinniness of his legs. Suddenly a lion came bounding toward him. The stag took off as fast as he could run and was soon far ahead of the lion as they raced across an open field. But when they came to a forest, the stag's antlers became entangled in the branches of the trees. The poor stag tried to pull himself free, but his antlers were stuck fast, and he soon fell victim to the teeth and claws of his enemy. "Woe is me!" he cried with his last breath. "I hated my legs, which could have saved my life, but I gloried in my horns, and they have caused my downfall."

*What is worth most is often valued least.*

# The Grasshopper and the Owl

An owl, who lived in a hollow tree, was in the habit of feeding by night and sleeping by day. But she found her sleep was being greatly disturbed by the chirping of a grasshopper living in the branches. The owl begged the grasshopper to have some consideration for her comfort, but if anything, he only chirped louder. At last the owl could not stand it any longer and was determined to rid herself of the pest by means of a trick. Speaking to the grasshopper, she said in her most pleasant voice, "As I cannot sleep because of your singing, which, believe me, is as sweet as the sound of a harp, I think I shall taste some of the wonderful nectar that I was given the other day. Won't you come in and join me?" The grasshopper was flattered by the praise of his song, and his mouth, too, watered at the mention of the delicious drink. "I would be delighted to join you," he said to the owl. No sooner had he gotten inside the hollow where the owl was sitting than she pounced upon him and ate him up.

*Beware of flattery and false invitations.*

# The Bear and the Bees

A bear was searching for berries in the woods when he came across an old log filled with honey. Wishing to find out whether any of the honey bees were at home, he cautiously sniffed around the log. A bee happened to be returning home from the fields with more honey. When he saw the bear, he angrily leaped upon his nose, stung him fiercely, and flew swiftly into his house. The wretched bear then rushed at the log with his teeth and claws, but the entire nest of bees poured out and swarmed all over him. Stumbling away in agony, the bear was only able to save himself by jumping headfirst into a nearby pond.

*Do not take what is not yours.*

# The Donkey, the Fox, and the Lion

A donkey and a fox who were friends decided to go off together to look for food. They had not gone far before they saw a lion coming their way, and they both became dreadfully frightened. But the fox had an idea to save his own skin. He went boldly up to the lion and whispered in his ear, "I'll help you get hold of the donkey without having to chase him down if you'll promise to let me go free." The lion agreed to this. The fox then went back to his companion the donkey and led him to a hidden pit that had been dug by some hunters as a trap for wild animals. He pushed the donkey into the pit. When the lion saw that the donkey was trapped and couldn't get away, he turned his attention first to the fox. After he had his fill of the wily fox, he then began to feast upon the donkey.

*Betray a friend, and you'll often find you have ruined yourself, too.*

# The Dog Chasing a Wolf

A dog was chasing a wolf. As the dog ran, he thought about what a fine fellow he was, what strong legs he had, and how quickly they raced along the ground. "Now, see that wolf," he said to himself, "what a poor creature he is. He is no match for me and he knows it. Look how he runs away!" But the wolf looked over his shoulder just then and said, "Don't you imagine I'm running away from you, my friend. It's your master, the hunter with the gun, that I'm afraid of."

*Don't fool yourself with illusions of power.*

# The Hunter and the Woodsman

A hunter was searching in the forest for the tracks of a lion. He noticed a woodcutter busy chopping down a tree. "Excuse me, sir," asked the hunter. "Have you noticed a lion's footprints anywhere around here? Or do you perhaps know where the lion's den might be?" "Surely," the woodcutter said. "If you will come with me, I will show you the lion himself." The hunter turned pale with fear, and his teeth chattered as he replied, "Oh, I'm not looking for the lion, thanks, but only for his tracks."

# The Old Lion and the Fox

A lion, feeble with age and no longer able to get food for himself by force, decided to do so by trickery. He went into a cave and lay down inside, pretending to be sick. Whenever any of the other animals entered to inquire after his health, he sprang upon them and devoured them. Many lost their lives in this way, until one day a fox came along and,

suspecting the truth, stayed safely outside the cave as he called, "How are you feeling, lion?" "Oh, dear me," replied the lion, "I am doing very poorly. But why do you stand outside? Please, come in." "I would have done so," answered the fox, "if I hadn't noticed that all the footprints point toward the cave and none the other way."

*It is wise to learn from the misfortunes of others.*

# The Tortoise and the Eagle

A tortoise, discontented with his lowly life and envious of the birds he saw enjoying themselves in the air, asked an eagle to teach him to fly. The eagle protested that it was useless for him to try, since nature had not given the tortoise any wings. But the tortoise begged the eagle and promised to reward him with great treasures. "It is just a question of learning how to fly," insisted the tortoise, so at last the eagle consented to do the best he could and picked him up in his talons. Soaring up to a great height in the sky, he then let the tortoise go. "Now fly, tortoise," commanded the eagle, but the wretched tortoise fell headlong into the sea.

*Be content with what you are.*

# The Wolf, the Mother, and Her Child

A hungry wolf was prowling about in search of food. By and by he heard the cries of a child coming from inside a little cottage. As he crouched beneath the window, he heard the mother say to the child, "Stop crying or I'll throw you to the wolf!" The wolf was delighted because he thought the mother really meant what she said. So he waited outside the window for a long, long time, expecting a fine meal. In the evening he heard the mother cuddling her child and saying, "If the naughty wolf comes, he shall not get my little one—Daddy will kill him." The wolf got up in disgust and walked away. "As for the people in that house," he said to himself, "you can't believe a word they say."

# The Lioness and the Fox

A lioness and a fox were talking together and bragging about their children, as mothers like to do. "All of my cubs are a joy to see," said the fox, and then she added, rather meanly, "but I notice you have only one baby." "That's true," said the lioness, "but that one is a lion."

*It's quality, not quantity, that counts.*

# The Gnat and the Lion

A gnat once went up to a lion and said, "I am not in the least afraid of you. I don't even think you are a match for me in strength, for what does strength mean, after all? Only that you can scratch with your claws and bite with your teeth. Why, that means nothing. I am stronger than you, and if you don't believe me, then let's fight and see!" Then the gnat darted in and bit the lion on the nose. When the lion felt the sting, in his rush to crush the little bug he scratched his own nose badly and began to bleed. The gnat was not hurt at all and buzzed off gloating over his victory. Soon afterward, however, the gnat got entangled in a spider's web and was caught and eaten by the spider. The little gnat that had triumphed over the King of Beasts fell prey to an insignificant insect.

# The Gnat and the Bull

A gnat landed on one of the horns of a bull and sat there for quite a while. When she felt that she had rested long enough and was ready to fly away, she said to the bull, "Do you mind if I go now?" The bull merely raised his eyes and answered, without interest, "It's all the same to me. I didn't notice when you came, and I won't care when you go away."

*We are of much more importance in our own eyes than in the eyes of our neighbors.*

# The Donkey, the Rooster, and the Lion

A donkey and a rooster were friends. Along came a fierce lion, who had been starving for days. The lion was just about to attack the donkey and make a meal of him when the rooster, rising to his full height and flapping his wings vigorously, uttered a tremendous crow. Now, if there is one thing that frightens a lion, some folks say, it is the crowing of a rooster. The minute the lion heard the noise, he ran off as fast as he could. The donkey was mightily pleased to see this. He thought to himself, "If a lion is scared of a rooster, he will be even more frightened by a donkey." So the donkey ran out and chased the lion. But as soon as they were out of sight of the rooster, the lion suddenly turned upon the donkey and ate him up.

*False confidence often leads to disaster.*

# The Fox and the Goat

A fox fell into a well and was unable to get out again. By and by a thirsty goat came along. "How is the water down there?" the goat asked. "Great!" said the fox. "It's the best water I ever tasted in all my life. Come on down and try it yourself." And without another thought, the goat jumped right in and began to drink. While the goat was drinking, the fox jumped onto the goat's back and from there was able to climb out of the well. Then he coolly began to walk away. "Hey," called the goat, suddenly realizing that he was stuck in the well, "what about me?" But the fox merely tossed his head and said, "If you had as much sense in your head as you have hair in your beard, you wouldn't have jumped into the well without being sure that you could get out again."

*Look before you leap.*

# The Heron

A heron went wading early one morning to fish for his breakfast in a shallow stream. There were many fish in the water, but the stately heron thought he could find better. "Such small fry is certainly not suitable fare for a heron," he remarked to himself. And as a choice young perch swam by, the heron tipped his long bill in the air and snapped, "No, sir, I certainly wouldn't open my beak for that!" The sun grew higher and all the fish left the shallows for the cool, deep middle of the stream. When the heron could find no trace of a fish left in the stream, he was very grateful to finally break his fast on a mere snail.

# The Mice in Council

Once upon a time all the mice called a meeting to decide upon the best way to protect themselves against the attacks of the cat. After several suggestions had been discussed, one of the mice got up and said, "I think I have hit upon a plan that will keep us safe in the future. We should fasten a bell around the neck of our enemy the cat. Then the tinkling of the bell will warn us whenever she is coming near, and we will have time to run and hide." This speech was enthusiastically applauded, and all the mice had agreed upon this plan when a wise old mouse stood up and said, "I agree with you all that this is an excellent idea, but may I ask which one of us is going to put the bell around the neck of the cat?"

*Some things are easier said than done.*

# Hercules and the Wagoner

A wagoner was driving his team of horses along a muddy lane when the wheels of his wagon sank so deep in the muck that his horses could not move them. As he stood there, looking helplessly at the mess and calling loudly to the god Hercules for assistance, the god himself appeared and said, "Put your shoulder to the wheel, man, and encourage your horses, and then you may call on me to help you. If you won't lift a finger to help yourself, you can't expect Hercules or anyone else to come to your aid."

*You must try to help yourself before you ask for assistance from others.*

# The Boastful Traveler

A man once traveled far and wide throughout the world, and when he returned home he was full of wonderful tales of the amazing things he had done in foreign countries. One of his favorite stories was about a jumping contest at Rhodes, in which, he bragged, he had jumped so far that no one could beat him. "Just go to Rhodes and ask them," he said. "Everyone will tell you it is true." But one of his listeners interrupted him, saying, "If you can jump as far as all that, we do not need to go to Rhodes to prove it. Just imagine for a minute that you are back in Rhodes. And now—jump!"

*Actions speak louder than words.*

# The Lion, Jupiter, and the Elephant

The lion, in spite of his great strength and sharp teeth, is a coward in one respect: he cannot bear the sound of a rooster crowing. A fierce lion was strolling along one day when he heard a loud "Cock-a-doodle-do!" The lion raced far into the woods in terror. Finally, he stopped, and he felt quite ashamed of himself for being so frightened. Just then he met an elephant. He noticed that the great beast kept his ears perked up all the time, as if he were listening for something, and he asked the elephant why he did so. Just then a gnat came humming by, and the elephant said, "Do you see that wretched little buzzing insect? I'm terribly afraid it will get into my ear, and if it does, I'm done for." The lion's spirits rose at once when he heard this. "Well," he said to himself, "if the elephant, huge as he is, is afraid of a tiny gnat, I need not be so ashamed of being afraid of a rooster, who is ten thousand times bigger than a gnat."

*Everything is relative.*

# The Rooster and the Jewel

A rooster, scratching the ground for something to eat, uncovered a beautiful jewel that had by chance been dropped there. "Ho!" said he. "A fine thing you are, no doubt. If your owner had found you, she would have been overjoyed. But for me—I am hungry. I would rather have a single kernel of corn than all the jewels in the world."

*What has great value to one person may be worthless to another.*

# The Father and His Sons

A man had four sons who were always quarreling with one another. Try as he might, he could not get his sons to live together in harmony. Finally, the man thought of a plan to convince his sons of their foolishness. "Fetch me a bundle of sticks," he commanded. "Now," he said to his youngest son, "break the bundle across your knees." "I cannot, Father," replied the boy. "It is much too difficult." Each son in turn tried to break the bundle of sticks across his knees. Of course, all of them failed. Then the father untied the bundle and handed each of his sons one stick. "Now break the sticks," he ordered. One by one, the sticks snapped easily. "You see, my boys," said the man, "united you will be more than a match for your enemies. But if you quarrel and separate, your weakness will put you at the mercy of those who attack you."

*Union is strength.*

# The Eagle and the Crow

One day a crow saw an eagle swoop down on a lamb and carry it aloft in its talons. "My word," said the crow. "I'll try that myself." So it flew high up into the air and then came shooting down with a great whirring of wings onto the back of a big ram, with the intention of carrying it off. The crow had no sooner landed than its claws got caught fast in the ram's wool, and nothing it could do was of any use. There it stuck, flapping away and only making things worse instead of better. By and by, along came the shepherd. "Aha," he said, "what do you think you're doing?" And he took the crow and clipped its wings and carried it home to his children. It looked so odd that they didn't know what to make of it. "What sort of bird is it, Father?" they asked. "It's a crow," he replied, "and nothing but a crow. But it wanted to be taken for an eagle."

*It's wise to know your own limitations.*

# The Donkey and His Purchaser

A farmer went to market to buy a donkey. When he found a beast that looked strong and healthy, he arranged with the owner to take the donkey home on trial to see what it was like. When the farmer got home, he put the donkey into his stable along with the others. The newcomer took a look around and immediately lay down next to the laziest and greediest beast in the stable. When the master saw this, he harnessed the donkey and took it right back to its owner. The owner was very surprised to see them back so soon and said, "What, do you mean to say you have tested him already?" "I don't need to put him through any more tests," replied the farmer. "I could see what sort of beast he was from the companion he picked for himself."

*You may be judged by the friends you choose.*

# The Two Bags

We all carry two bags around with us, one in front and one behind. Both are packed full of faults. The bag in front contains our neighbors' faults; the one behind us contains our own faults. And that is why we do not see our own faults, but we never fail to see those of others.

# The Milkmaid and Her Pail

A farmer's daughter finished milking the cows and was carrying her pail of milk upon her head. As she walked along, she started to daydream: "The milk in this pail will provide me with cream. I will make the cream into butter and take it to the market to. sell. With the money, I will buy some eggs, and these will hatch into chickens. Then I'll sell some of the chickens, and with the money I'll buy myself a beautiful new dress, which I will wear to the dance. All the young fellows will admire me and want to dance with me, but I'll just toss my head and have nothing to say to them." At this, she forgot all about the pail on her head, and imagining herself at the dance, she tossed her head. Down went the pail, the milk spilled out all over the ground, and all her fine plans vanished in a moment!

*Do not count your chickens before they are hatched.*

# The Two Goats

Two proud goats happened to arrive at the same time at the peaks of opposite cliffs in a mountain range. Between the cliffs, a fierce river ran through the rocky valley. The only bridge across this great chasm was a fallen tree so narrow that two small animals could hardly pass each other at the same time. But these two big goats were very stubborn, and each felt that he had the right to cross the river first; so setting one hoof at time upon the slender log, they found themselves head to head in the middle of the bridge. Neither goat would let the other pass, and finally they both fell headlong into the roaring waters below.

*If you won't compromise in a disagreement, you may both lose.*

# The Farmer and the Fox

A farmer was greatly annoyed by a fox who came prowling about his yard at night and carried off his chickens. So he set a trap and caught the fox. Then the farmer tied a bunch of dried grass to the fox's tail, set fire to it, and let him go. Unfortunately for the farmer, the fox headed straight for the fields where the corn was ripe and ready for cutting. Everything quickly caught fire and burned, and the unlucky farmer lost his whole harvest.

*Revenge is a two-edged sword.*

# The Man and the Lion

A man and a lion were companions on a journey. After a while they began to brag about themselves, with each claiming to be superior to the other in strength and courage. They were still arguing when they came to a stone statue showing a man strangling a lion. "There!" said the man triumphantly. "Look at that! Doesn't it prove to you that people are stronger than lions?" "Not so fast, my friend," said the lion. "That is only your view of the situation. If we lions could carve stone, you can be sure that in all of our statues you would see the man being beaten by the lion!"

*There are two sides to every question.*

# The Boys and the Frogs

Some mischievous boys were playing on the edge of a pond when they noticed some frogs swimming about in the shallow water. The boys began to amuse themselves by pelting the frogs with stones, and they killed several of them. At last one of the frogs stuck his head out of the water and cried, "Oh, stop! Please stop! I beg of you—what you consider a game is death to us."

# The Wolf and the Crane

A wolf once got a bone stuck in his throat. Choking, he went to a crane and begged her to stick her long bill down his throat and pull it out. "I'll make it worth your while," the wolf said. The crane did as she was asked and got the bone out quite easily. The wolf thanked her warmly and was just turning away when the crane cried, "What about my reward?" "Well, what about it?" snapped the wolf, baring his teeth as he spoke. "You can go about boasting that you once put your head into a wolf's mouth and didn't get it bitten off. What more do you want?"

*When you serve the wicked, you can expect no reward.*

# The Goose That Laid the Golden Eggs

A man and his wife were amazed to discover that their goose had laid an egg of solid gold. The next day the goose laid another golden egg, and the next day another! The man and his wife knew they were very lucky, but they were greedy, too, and they soon decided that they were not getting rich fast enough. "Why, this bird must be filled with golden eggs!" they cried. "We don't have to wait for just one each day. Let's kill her and get all the precious eggs at once." But when they cut the goose open, they found she was just like any other goose. So they did not get rich all at once, as they had hoped, and they did not get any more golden eggs.

*Being greedy can made you lose everything.*

# The Fox and the Leopard

A fox and a leopard were arguing about their looks. Each claimed to be the more handsome of the two. The leopard said, "Look at my beautiful coat. You have nothing to match that." But the fox replied, "Your coat may be beautiful, but my brains are smarter still."

*Wisdom is worth more than beauty.*

# The Miser

A miser sold everything he had and bought gold coins. Then he melted down all the gold into a single lump, which he buried secretly in a field. Every day he went to look at it. Sometimes he spent hours gloating over his treasure. "Where is my boss sneaking off to every day?" wondered one of his workmen, so the man followed the miser and spied the hidden treasure. That night the man dug up the gold lump and stole it. When the miser went to visit his treasure the next day, he discovered that it was gone. The miser was beside himself, tearing out his hair and screaming in fury. "What on earth has happened?" asked his neighbor. "My gold! My gold!" cried the miser and he told of his misfortune. "Don't be so upset," said the neighbor. "Put a brick into the hole and take a look at it every day. You won't be any worse off than before, for even when you had your gold it was of no earthly use to you."

*Money has no true value if it is not used.*

# The Beekeeper

One day, while the beekeeper was out, a thief stole all the honey from the beehives. When the beekeeper returned, he was so upset that he just stood there staring in shock at the empty hives. Before long the bees came back from gathering honey. When they saw their hives bare and the beekeeper standing by, they went after him viciously with their stings. At this he cried out, "You ungrateful scoundrels. You don't even look for the thief who stole my honey, and then you go and sting me, even though I have always taken such good care of you!"

*When you hit back, make sure you are striking the right person.*

# The Slave and the Lion

In Rome in ancient times, a slave ran away from his cruel master. To avoid being captured, he ran into the desert. As he wandered about in search of food and shelter, he came to a cave that appeared to be empty. Really, however, it was a lion's den, and almost immediately, to the horror of the poor runaway, the lion himself appeared. The slave expected the lion to spring on him and devour him. Instead, to the man's utter astonishment, the lion limped over, whining and lifting up his paw. The paw was swollen and inflamed from a large thorn embedded in the ball of the foot. The man removed the thorn and cleaned the wound as best he could. In time, the lion's foot healed completely. The lion's gratitude was unbounded. He looked upon the man as his friend, and they shared the cave for some time.

A day came, however, when the slave began to long for the company of other people, so he said farewell to the lion and returned to the town. Here he was soon recognized and carried off in chains to his former master. "This runaway slave must be punished," said his master. "He shall be thrown to the lions tomorrow in the public theater!" The next day, the lions were set loose in the arena. Among them was one particularly huge and ferocious beast. Then the poor slave was thrown into the ring. Imagine the amazement of the spectators when the enormous lion, after one glance, bounded up to the slave and lay down at his feet with every expression of affection and delight! It was his old friend from the cave! The audience clamored that the slave's life should be spared, and the governor of the town, marveling at such gratitude and loyalty in a beast, decreed that both should be set free.

*One good turn deserves another.*

# The Wolf and the Lamb

A wolf came upon a lamb straying from the flock and didn't want to take the life of so helpless a creature without a good excuse. So the wolf said, "You are the lamb that insulted me last year." "That is impossible, sir," bleated the lamb, "for I wasn't even born then." "Well," retorted the wolf, "you eat from my pastures." "That cannot be," replied the lamb, "for I have never yet tasted grass." "You drink from my spring, then," continued the wolf. "Indeed, sir," said the poor lamb, "I have never yet drunk anything but my mother's milk." "Well, anyhow," said the wolf, "I'm not going without my dinner," and he sprang upon the lamb and devoured it without another word.

*A tyrant needs no excuse.*

# The Miller, His Son, and Their Donkey

A miller, accompanied by his young son, was walking his donkey to market to sell it. Along the road they met some girls, laughing and talking. "Did you ever see such a pair of fools?" they said. "To be trudging along the dusty road when they could be riding!" The miller thought there was sense in what they said, so he sat his son upon the donkey, and he walked alongside. Soon they met some old men, who greeted them and said, "You'll spoil that son of yours, letting him ride while you walk on foot! Make that lazybones walk! It will do him good." So the miller traded places with his son. Now the father rode and the son walked. They had not gone far when they came upon a group of women and children. "What a selfish man!" they said. "Look how he rides in comfort while he makes his poor little boy follow as best he can on his own legs!" So the miller lifted his son up behind him on the donkey. Down the road they met some travelers, who asked, "Is that your own donkey, or did you hire the beast for a ride to market?" "It is mine," replied the miller. "I'm on my way to market to sell it." The travelers were quick with an opinion: "Good heavens," they said, "with a load like that the poor beast will be so exhausted by the time he gets there that no one will look at him. Why, you'd do better to carry him!" "Anything to please you," said the miller. He and his son climbed down, tied the donkey's legs together with a rope, and slung him on a pole. Carrying him between them, they at last approached the town and began to cross the bridge to the market. When the townspeople saw this ridiculous sight, they gathered in crowds to laugh at the father and son. The donkey became frightened by all the noise. He kicked and struggled until the ropes that bound him broke. The poor donkey then fell into the water and drowned. So the unfortunate miller and his son walked all the way home.

*When you try to please everyone, you end up pleasing no one.*

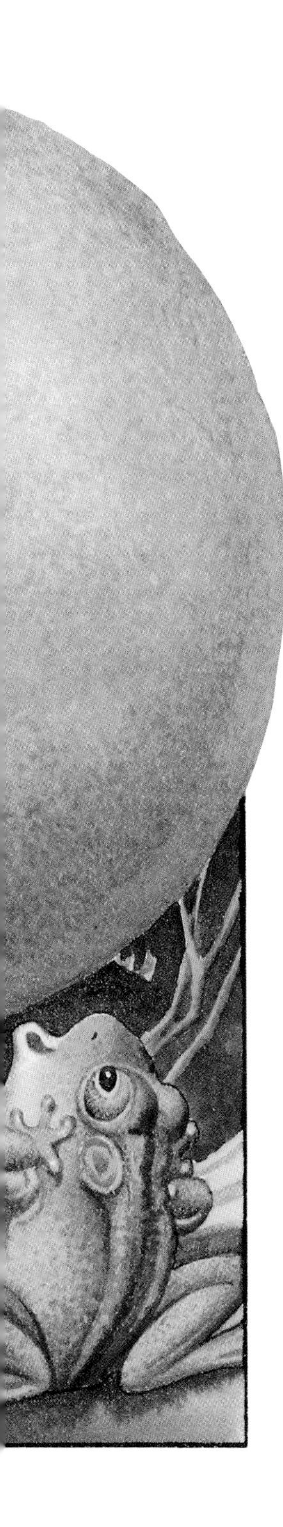

# The Ox and the Frog

Two little frogs were playing at the edge of a pool when an ox came down to the water to drink. By accident, the ox stepped on one of the frogs and crushed him. Sad and sorry, the other little frog returned home. "Where is your brother?" asked his mother. "He is dead, Mother," said the little frog. "An enormous big creature with four legs came to our pool this morning and trampled him down in the mud." "Enormous, was he? Was he as big as this?" said the frog, puffing herself out to look as big as possible. "Oh, yes, much bigger," was the answer. The frog puffed herself out still more. "Was he as big as this?" said she. "Oh, yes, Mother, MUCH bigger," said the little frog. And yet again she puffed and puffed herself out until she was almost as round as a ball. "Stop, Mother. Do not puff yourself out any more than that!" said the little frog. "Do not be angry, but you would burst before you could successfully imitate the hugeness of that creature."

*Self-conceit may lead to self-destruction.*

# The Grasshopper and the Ants

One fine day in winter some ants were busy drying off their store of corn, which had gotten rather damp during a long rainfall. Along came a grasshopper who begged them to spare her a few grains. "For," she said, "I'm simply starving." The ants stopped working for a moment, although this was against their principles. "May we ask," said they, "what you were doing with yourself all last summer? Why didn't you collect enough food for the winter, as we did?" "The fact is," replied the grasshopper, "I was so busy singing that I hadn't the time." "If you spent the summer singing," said the ants, "you can't do better than to spend the winter dancing." And they chuckled and went on with their work.

*It is best to prepare today for the needs of tomorrow.*

# The Lion, the Fox, and the Stag

A lion lay sick in his den, unable to hunt for food. So he said to his friend the fox: "My good friend, I wish you would go to the forest and persuade the big stag, who lives there, to come to my den. I am hungry for a stag's heart and brain." The fox went into the woods and found the stag. "My dear sir," the fox said, "you're in luck. You know the lion, our king? Well, he is about to die and has appointed you to rule over the beasts after his death. I hope you won't forget that I was the first to bring you the good news. And now I must go back to him. If you will take my advice, you will come too and thank him personally." The stag was highly flattered and, suspecting nothing, followed the fox to the lion's den. No sooner was he inside than the lion sprang upon him, but the stag took off in a flash and escaped to the woods with only his ears torn.

The lion was terribly disappointed, for he was very hungry in spite of his illness. So he begged the fox to have another try at coaxing the stag to his den. "It will be almost impossible this time," said the fox, "but I'll try." Off he went to the woods a second time and found the stag resting and trying to recover from his fright. As soon as he saw the fox, the stag cried, "You scoundrel, what do you mean by trying to lure me to my death like that? Get out of here or I'll gore you to death with my horns." But the wily fox merely answered, "What a coward you were. Surely you didn't think the lion meant any harm? Why, he was only going to whisper some royal secrets into your ear, but you went running off like a scared rabbit. You have rather disgusted him, and I wouldn't be surprised if he makes the wolf king instead—unless you come back at once and apologize. I promise you he won't hurt you."

The stag was foolish enough to be persuaded to return to the lion's cave. This time the lion quickly overpowered him and feasted royally. The fox watched carefully, and when the lion wasn't looking, the fox leaned over and gobbled up the stag's brain himself. Soon the lion began searching for the brain, without success, of course. The fox, who was looking on, said, "I don't think there's much use in looking for the brain. A creature who twice walked into a lion's den can't possible have had any."

# The Hound and the Hare

A young hound was teasing a hare. Sometimes he would catch her and snap at her with his teeth as though he were about to kill her. At other times he would let her free and frisk about her, as if he were playing with another dog. At last the hare said, "I wish you would show yourself in your true colors! If you are my friend, why do you bite me? If you are my enemy, why do you play with me?"

*He is no friend who plays double.*

# The Farmer and Fortune

A farmer was plowing his field one day when he unearthed a pot of golden coins. He was overjoyed at his discovery, and from that day on he gave thanks to the Goddess of the Earth. Fortune was displeased at this and came to him, saying, "Why do you give Earth credit for the gift that I gave to you? You never thought of thanking me for your good luck, and yet I know that if you were suddenly to lose this pot of gold you would be quick to blame me, Fortune, for your bad luck.

*Give thanks where thanks are due.*

# The Bear and the Travelers

Two travelers were walking down the road together when they suddenly saw a bear ahead of them. Before the bear saw them, one of the men quickly climbed up into a tree and hid. The other was not as nimble as his companion. He knew he could not escape in time, so he threw himself on the ground and pretended to be dead. The bear came up and sniffed all around him, but the man kept perfectly still and held his breath, for he had heard that a bear will not touch a dead body. The bear was fooled and went away. When the coast was clear, the traveler in the tree came down. "What did the bear whisper when he put his mouth to your ear?" he asked his companion. The other replied, "He told me never again to travel with a friend who deserts you at the first sign of danger."

*Misfortune tests the sincerity of friendship.*

# The Crow and the Swan

A crow was filled with envy on seeing the beautiful white feathers of a swan. "It must be the water in which the swan constantly bathes and swims that gives her such lovely plumage," thought the crow. So he left his own neighborhood, where he always found plenty to eat from the scraps of the townspeople, and he went to live among the pools and streams in the country. But even though he bathed and washed his feathers many times a day, he didn't make them any whiter, and after a while he died of hunger.

*You may change your habits but not your nature.*

# The Horse and His Rider

A young man, who considered himself quite an excellent horseman, jumped onto the back of a very lively horse. As soon as the horse felt the weight of the man in the saddle, he started to gallop—and the man could do nothing to stop him. As they raced down the road, someone called out to the rider, "Say, where are you off to in such a hurry?" "I have no idea," the man replied, and then he pointed to the horse: "Ask him!"

# The Lion and the Three Bulls

A lion watched three bulls grazing in a meadow. The lion longed to go after them, but he knew that he was no match for the three as long as they stayed together. So he began starting false rumors about them, whispering nasty secrets to create jealousies and distrust among the bulls. This plan succeeded so well that before long the bulls grew cold and unfriendly and finally began to avoid each other and graze in separate parts of the meadow. As soon as the lion saw this, he fell upon them one by one and devoured each in turn.

*United we stand, divided we fall:*
*the quarrels of friends are the opportunities of enemies.*

# The Wolf and the Sheep

A wolf was attacked and badly bitten by some dogs and lay a long time by the side of the road. After a while he began to revive, and, feeling very hungry, he called out to a passing sheep: "Would you kindly bring me some water from the stream nearby? I can manage to get some meat, if only I could get something to drink." But this sheep was no fool. "I can quite understand," he replied, "that if I brought you the water, you would have no difficulty getting the meat. Good-bye."

*It's wise to keep a safe distance from your enemies.*

# The Donkey in the Lion's Skin

A donkey found a lion's skin and dressed himself in it. Then he went about frightening everyone he met, for they all believed he was a lion and fled in terror when they saw him coming. Delighted with the success of his trick, he brayed loudly in triumph. The fox heard him, recognized him at once for the donkey he was, and said, "Oh, my friend, it's you, is it? I, too, would have been afraid if I hadn't heard your voice."

*Clothes can disguise a fool—until he opens his mouth.*

# The Stag and the Lion

A stag who was being chased by the hounds ran into a cave, where he hoped to be safe. Unfortunately, the cave was the home of a lion, who licked his lips hungrily when he saw the stag. "I am so unhappy," cried the stag. "I am saved from the fury of the dogs only to fall into the clutches of a lion."

*Out of the frying pan, into the fire.*

# The Wolf and the Horse

A wolf was rambling about when he came to a field of oats. Now, wolves do not eat oats, so he was about to continue on his way when he met a horse. "Look," said the wolf. "Here's a fine field of oats. For your sake I have left it untouched, and I shall greatly enjoy hearing the sound of your teeth munching the ripe grain." But the horse replied, "If wolves could eat oats, my fine friend, you would hardly have sacrificed your belly for the pleasure of hearing me eat."

*There is no virtue in giving to others something that is useless to you.*

# The Goatherd and the Goat

A goatherd was gathering his flock to return to the barn when one of his goats strayed off and refused to join the others. The goatherd tried for a long time to get her to follow him by calling and whistling to her, but the goat took no notice of him at all. So at last he threw a stone at her and broke one of her horns. In dismay, the goatherd begged her not to tell his master, but she replied, "You silly fellow, he would see my horn even if I held my tongue."

*It's no use trying to hide what cannot be hidden.*

# The Hare and the Tortoise

The hare was always bragging about his fantastic speed, claiming that no one could ever beat him in a race. One day he started taunting the tortoise: "You are so slow on your feet. You must be the slowest of everyone." "Just you wait," said the tortoise. "I'll run a race with you, and I'll wager that I win." "Oh, really," replied the hare, who was quite amused at the idea. "Let's try and see." So they agreed that the fox should set up the race and be the judge. When the fox said "Go!" the tortoise and the

hare started off side by side. But the hare was soon so far ahead that he thought he might as well take a rest, so he lay down on the grass and fell fast asleep. Meanwhile, the tortoise kept plodding on and on until he eventually reached the finish line. At last the hare woke up with a start and dashed forward at his fastest pace. But he was too late, for he found that the tortoise had already won the race.

*Slow and steady wins the race.*

# Index